ARION AND THE DOLPHIN

Arion and the dolphin is an opera in 9 scenes for
professional and community performers. The
music is composed by Alec Roth and the
libretto is by Vikram Seth. It was
commissioned by the Baylis Programme at
English National Opera.

By the same author

MAPPINGS (verse)

THE GOLDEN GATE : A NOVEL IN VERSE

THE HUMBLE ADMINISTRATOR'S GARDEN (verse)

ALL YOU WHO SLEEP TONIGHT (verse)

THREE CHINESE POETS (translations)

FROM HEAVEN LAKE : TRAVELS THROUGH SINKIANG AND TIBET

A SUITABLE BOY

BEASTLY TALES FROM HERE AND THERE (verse)

ARION &
the DOLPHIN

A LIBRETTO BY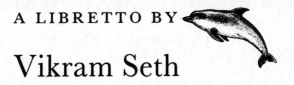
Vikram Seth

PHOENIX HOUSE, LONDON

The right of Vikram Seth to be identified
as the author of this work has been
asserted by him in accordance with the
Copyright, Designs and Patents Act 1988.

First published in Great Britain in 1994 by
Phoenix House
An imprint of Orion Books Ltd
Orion House, 5 Upper St Martin's Lane,
London WC2H 9EA

Arion and the Dolphin was commissioned by the Baylis Programme with funds
provided by the Arts Council of Great Britain

A CIP catalogue record for this book is
available from the British Library

ISBN 8975 8046 0

Typeset by Deltatype Ltd, Ellesmere Port, S. Wirral
Printed in Great Britain by Butler & Tanner Ltd, Frome & London

For the wild dolphin, 'Fungie'

Irish dolphin, swift and single,
Dwelling off the coast of Dingle,
Choosing now and then to mingle
   With the flipperless and glum,
Bringing wonder and elation
To our jaded human nation,
I present you this creation
   Of my fingers and my thumb.

THE 9 SCENES RUN INTO EACH OTHER IN A CONTINUOUS ACTION

PRINCIPALS (professional performers)

PERIANDER, Tyrant of Corinth	tenor
ARION, his young court musician	lyric-baritone
CAPTAIN of the ship	bass-baritone
THE DOLPHIN	mezzo-soprano

CHORUS (community performers: adults, young people and children)

GUARDS	AUDIENCE
THE SEA	DOLPHINS
SAILORS	SEA-CREATURES
SICILIANS.	FISHERFOLK
MUSICIANS	PEOPLE OF CORINTH
DANCERS	

the following solo roles should be taken by members of the chorus:

MASTER OF CEREMONIES	spoken role
1ST MUTINEER	baritone
2ND MUTINEER	tenor
MESSENGER	boy soprano

Scene 1

Corinth. A courtyard under the stars. Arion is lying asleep on the ground beside a couch. His dreams are troubled and he wakes with a start.

PERIANDER *shouting from offstage:*
Arion! Arion!

Arion gets up hurriedly, adjusts his clothes and stands behind the couch holding his lyre. Periander marches in with his guards.

PERIANDER:
Arion! What's all this I hear about your wanting to go to Sicily for some music festival?

ARION:
Well –

PERIANDER:
I won't have it.

ARION:
But –

PERIANDER:
Do you think I don't know what is going on behind my back?

ARION:

I only thought –

PERIANDER:

Don't interrupt! And don't deny it either.

ARION:

But I didn't –

PERIANDER:

You cannot go, and that is that.

Arion begins to strum the lyre.

PERIANDER:

    Arion,
Think of my court, of Corinth, and of me.

ARION:

I do, my lord.
Yours is the only home that I have known
Since I was a boy, parentless and alone.
I do not gladly leave it empty of song.

PERIANDER:

Good.

ARION:

Sir, let me go to Sicily.
I will be back before long.
I'll sing more freely when I'm free.

PERIANDER:

What? Do you talk of tyranny?

Go! go!

I do not know why I should love you so.

I have two sons, one is a dolt, his brother

Hates me and flees me, claiming I killed his mother.

The rabble hate me, blood clings to my hands –

The blood of this, the blood of many lands.

My silent mentor used his stick to lop

The tallest stalks of corn from every crop;

So all of any weight or excellence

In Corinth have been killed or driven hence.

Do you not fear me, Periander, Tyrant of Corinth?

ARION:

It is the dearest of my aims,

My lord, to quell such wild and unjust claims.

In Sicily, my lord, all men will know

Your greatness, for my songs will tell them so.

Let me take part, and let me spread your fame,

Lord Periander, when I sing your name.

PERIANDER:

And are you sure you'll win? If not, you'll die.

Pause

Go, go. Leave my court in silence.

As Periander leaves, Arion looks up at the night sky.

ARION:
>Bright stars, bring comfort
>To those who dream.
>Bright stars, guide me to fame
>By land, by sea –
>So that my form and name
>May rest among you in the sky –
>Bright, constant stars,
>That I, like you,
>May never fade or die.
>And you, dark, restless sea
>Be gentle on my way
>From Greece to Sicily.

Scene 2

As Arion sings to the sea, the Captain and the sailors appear, and begin to sing; and the scene changes to shipboard.

CAPTAIN:

Dark, restless sea,
Blue, green, grey, black –
Be gentle on our track
And grace my crew and me.
   Poseidon, bless my ship
   That we may rise and dip,
   Sailing with rapid clip
From Greece to Sicily.

SAILORS:

Dark, restless sea,
Black, grey, blue, green –
Our decks are scrubbed and clean –
Our ropes run strong and free.
   Fair winds, fill out our sails –
   Bring us no gusts or gales –
   Keep us from sharks and whales
From Greece to Sicily.

Arion!

Let's hear you sing!

Sing for your supper!

ARION *and the* SAILORS:

    Dark, restless sea,

    Blue, green, black, grey –

    Be gentle on my way

    From Greece to Sicily.

        May no storm shake the sky,

        Or seagulls wheel and cry,

        But dolphins dip and fly

    Beside my ship and me.

CAPTAIN:

Well, with a voice like that, I'm not surprised Periander did not want to let you go. How did your tune catch up with ours?

ARION:

I care about time and timing, Captain: it is the heart of my music.

CAPTAIN:

That's true for us as well. You'd make a good sailor.

ARION:

I'd make a terrible sailor – ninety-nine oars pulling one way, and one in the other.

CAPTAIN *laughs and takes his hands:*

Those hands would grow callussed too quickly anyway.

You're best doing what you do, Arion. In your profession, if the risks are greater, so are the rewards.

ARION:
What rewards?

CAPTAIN:
Why? Aren't you rich? Hasn't your singing brought you wealth?

ARION:
In my own right, this lyre is all I have. And what risks?

CAPTAIN:
Well, Periander has threatened you with death if you lose in the Sicilian festival.

ARION:
Periander –

CAPTAIN:
He is an unhappy man.

ARION:
Well, he certainly doesn't have much of a family life.

CAPTAIN:
He is alone, and at a fearful height.

ARION:
But many people are alone.
And you, Captain – do you have a family life? Or is your crew your family?

CAPTAIN:

My crew lead a hard life.

They care for silver, bronze, and when they get it, gold.

I care for them, perhaps they care for me.

I work them hard, they never mutiny.

I think I know their ways.

For more than half my nights and days

They are my family.

ARION:

But what of land, of Corinth, towards which you often gaze?

CAPTAIN:

You read my heart, Arion, through my eyes.

I have a house on shore

Not far from Corinth harbour, made of stone:

A laurel bush, some flowers, olive trees;

And there, when this good ship is on the seas,

My wife and my three daughters live alone

For many months, for years,

In peacetime and in war.

When I return, my wife is at the door.

I wipe away her tears.

I soothe her fears

With gifts and practicalities.

My daughters laugh to see me.

I chase them and they flee me.

The weeks fly by; then trade or battle draw

Me once more down to shore

To take sad leave of my sad wife and daughters

And change untrembling land for trembling waters.

ARION:

Have you no son to help you on the sea?

CAPTAIN *giving Arion a conch-shell:*

Arion, keep this shell.
It is a gift from me,
So guard it well.
It will make music in your ear
Whenever you choose to hear
The ocean's surge, its rustling harmony.
Arion, keep this shell.
Be well, be well.
The days have passed in talk, and now I see
The distant citadel,
The crags of Sicily.

Scene 3

As the ship approaches Sicily, or Sicily the ship, a crowd of Sicilians – villagers and petty tradesmen – appears on shore, singing an idiotic song.

SICILIANS:
Si-ci-ly, Si-ci-ly,
Such a pretty, gritty, witty co-un-tree.
Si-ci-ly, Si-ci-ly,
Won't you buy a little souvenir from me.

CAPTAIN:
What is the meaning of this silly ditty?
Where's the official welcoming committee?

SICILIAN:
Your boat arrived early. None of the officials is awake yet.

SICILIAN:
Hangovers.

SICILIAN:
Pre-festival festivities.

SICILIAN:
So who've you got on board that's so important anyway?

CAPTAIN:

The winner of your festival, for one.

SICILIAN:

What do you mean? Who do you mean?

CAPTAIN:

Arion – he'll teach you Sicilians how to sing.

SICILIANS:

Arion!

SICILIAN:

We've got good musicians too, you know. What do you think
this is, a backwater?

CAPTAIN:

No, no, far from it.

SICILIAN:

Welcome, Arion of Corinth.

SICILIAN:

Of Lesbos – he's from Lesbos.

SICILIAN:

Nonsense. He's from Corinth – his patron is Coriander.

SICILIAN:

Periander.

SICILIAN:

The one who killed his wife?

SICILIAN:

Or so they say.

CAPTAIN:

He's here to represent Periander.

SICILIAN:

Well, he'd better be good, then – or else he'll be for the chop.

SICILIAN:

He's from Lesbos. Ask him. Go on, ask him.

SICILIAN:

Ask him yourself.

SICILIAN:

I don't need to. Welcome, Arion of Lesbos.

ARION *sings beautifully:*

Thank you, citizens of Sicily.

The Sicilians are enchanted, and applaud him.

CAPTAIN:

Arion, I must go now. I will return from Italy in a few days to
take you home. Till then –

ARION:

But the competition – the festival – will you not be there? Will
you not hear me sing?

CAPTAIN:

Some other time, my friend, some other time.
I'll hear you sing when I have leisure from my trade.
But now it's business before pleasure, I'm afraid.

ARION:

Farewell. *Picks up his lyre, forgets the conch-shell.*

CAPTAIN:

Your shell. Do not forget your shell.

ARION:

It is a gift from you,
I'll guard it well.

SICILIAN:

He does have a nice voice.

SICILIAN:

Let's take him off to have a good time in the town.

SICILIAN:

Wine, women and song – off to the tavern with him.

SICILIAN:

A proper booze-up!

ARION:

Wonderful! Wonderful! A wonderful idea!

SICILIAN:

But what about practising for the festival?

SICILIAN:

It's in two days – just two days.

ARION:

Oh – there'll be plenty of time to practise –
But now it's pleasure before business, I'm afraid.

Laughing, the Sicilians take Arion off to have a good time.

_Scene 4 _

MASTER OF CEREMONIES:
And now, my lords, ladies and gentlemen, I present to you
Arion of Lesbos, Chief Musician at the court of Periander of
Corinth, master of the lyre –

Applause. Arion does not appear. General consternation.

MASTER OF CEREMONIES:
Arion of Lesbos, poet, singer, voice of Apollo incarnate,
discoverer of the tragic mode –

Desultory applause. Arion does not appear.

SICILIAN:
Etcetera, etcetera – but where's the singer?

SICILIAN:
Oh, he got drunk – he's probably sleeping it off –

SICILIAN:
That sleep will cost him his head.

SICILIAN:
And he didn't practise at all!

SICILIAN:
Too much wine and women, not enough song.

And now, ladies and gentlemen, for a learned and
discriminating audience like yourselves, I present the singer of
superb salutations to the royal ruler of cultured Corinth, the
tender but tenacious Tyrant –

laughter and jeers from the audience

– I introduce to you Arion of Lesbos, lyricist of lugubrious
lushness, fleetly flying on fluent feet, whose delightful daring
with Dionysian dithyrambs has captured and enraptured the
courts and colonies of Greece – who will now sing a song of
praise to his munificent and magnificent patron, the puissant
and paternal Periander – Arion of Lesbos!

*A Sicilian points out Arion, who is sleeping off his revelry behind an olive
tree. Arion, awake, looks troubled and afraid. He takes up his lyre, but
puts it down again. The audience variously splutters its ridicule and
mutters its disapproval. He covers his head with his hands. He tries
again, but all that comes out of his mouth is:*

ARION *to the tune of the* Si-ci-ly *song:*
   Pe-ri-ander, Pe-ri-ander

which he repeats helplessly.

*Then, panicking at the thought of the future wrath of Periander, he
fumbles for another tune:*

   Bright stars, bring comfort –

but he can get nowhere beyond this line.

SICILIAN:
How pathetic!

MASTER OF CEREMONIES:
According to the rules, Arion, two false starts is all you get.
Sing one last time, and then no more.

SICILIAN:
The third start is the last. Then he is doomed.

ARION:
Oh gods! My art deserts me. Untrouble my heart – fill with
your inspiration my empty shell –

*At the word, he thinks of the shell the Captain gave him, grasps it, and
puts it to his ear.*

Sounds of the sea are heard, and grow louder; the cries of dolphins too.

*He begins to strum his lyre, first slowly, then faster and faster until he
is lost in a frenzied song of virtuosity and emotion.*

*Sometimes he blows his conch, sometimes he thumps it. The words he
sings to are mainly fragmentary phrases, cries like 'Aaaaah', and
nonsensical syllables. Most of them have to do with the sea, but form no
coherent structure.*

SICILIAN:
He is crazed. Stop him.

SICILIAN:
No, no, no, let him sing –

SICILIAN:
The gods have blessed him with their madness.

The audience have risen and are singing, dancing and stomping around. At the end of the chant, Arion is the winner by acclamation.

Gold coins and gold dust rain down. Gold gifts and other precious objects are offered to him. A golden lyre – a golden robe. An adoring girl touches him and gives him her golden chain.

Arion is delighted, and beams at the pile of gold glittering in the centre of the stage.

SICILIANS:

More! More! Another song!

MASTER OF CEREMONIES:

Sing, Arion, sing once more! Sing for us once more! Stay in Sicily – stay with us for ever. Or at least sing us one last song before you go.

ARION *picks up the lyre and sings in a quieter strain:*

Dark restless sea,
Black, green, grey, blue,
Over whose waves I flew
To sing in Sicily,
   Accept my weight once more
   As gently as before.
   Bear me to Corinth shore
Alive, and safe, and free.

Scene 5

The ship at sea. It is night. The stars shine above. The gold glitters below. Arion is on the afterdeck. He looks up at the stars, smiles, stretches and yawns, then falls asleep. The sailors emerge from the shadows and gather round Arion's treasure.

SAILORS *awed:*
Look at that – look at that gold –

1ST MUTINEER:
And all that for a song.

SAILOR:
A single song.

1ST MUTINEER:
A single song
Gave him more than we earn our whole lives long.

CAPTAIN *who has been watching, unseen:*
Enough of this –

1ST MUTINEER:
Tell me the reason why
We who bore him across the sea
Should not share in his fortune equally?

SAILORS:
That's right – why not? –

2ND MUTINEER *stepping forward:*
That's fair by me.
Without our help where would Arion be?
Without hard hands could soft hands strum the lyre?

SAILORS:
Look at the gold dust glittering like fire.

2ND MUTINEER:
Give us that gold –

1ST MUTINEER:
    – or we will mutiny.

CAPTAIN:
You rogues – this gold has bent your brains.
He won it by his pains.

1ST MUTINEER:
What pains? A single song?

SAILORS:
A single song
Gave him more than we earn our whole lives long
With sinew and with sweat.

2ND MUTINEER:
Captain – do not forget
You have a house, and we have huts and shacks.

1ST MUTINEER:
This gold will help to paper up the cracks
Through which the wind knifes through
In hard midwinter, piercing us, not you.

MUTINEERS:
But join with us, and you can share this fortune too.

CAPTAIN:
I will not touch that gold for anything.

2ND MUTINEER:
Here, Captain, here's a ring.

CAPTAIN:
Not on your life —

2ND MUTINEER:
If you don't like it, give it to your wife.

CAPTAIN *flinging it away:*
Never!

1ST MUTINEER *snatching a sword from the pile, and holding it to the Captain's throat:*
Captain, be reasonable. Do not die.
I'm sure your wife would wish you to comply.

MUTINEERS:
Her golden-dusted dreams are all about you.
What would she do without you?

to the sailors
Let's take the gold
And stack it in the hold.
The Captain stays inside his room on board;
And when the gold is stored,
We'll deal with other things –

Arion sings out in his sleep.

SAILOR:
Listen – Arion sings –

2ND MUTINEER:
What of Arion?

1ST MUTINEER:
– Death.

CAPTAIN:
No!

1ST MUTINEER:
          Captain, save your breath.
Think of your family.

CAPTAIN:
I cannot bear the pain
That they should wait for me and not see me again.

1ST MUTINEER *shouting to the sailors:*
Take the gold!

Led by the mutineers, the sailors break open Arion's treasure and start to divide it among themselves. They sing the earlier words of the mutineers to justify their actions.

SAILOR:
Gold . . . the glittering gold . . .

CAPTAIN:
What shall I do?
What can I do?

   It's not the gods
      But our own hearts
         We need to fear.
     The evil starts
   Against all odds
        Not there but here.

Arion appears. A sudden silence.

ARION:
Captain, you are ill. What's happening? You look pale. What is all this?

CAPTAIN:
Arion, you must die.

Arion laughs, then realises that the Captain is serious.

ARION:
Captain –

CAPTAIN:
We much regret, Arion, that you must die.

ARION:
What is my crime? Tell me the reason why.

CAPTAIN:

You are too rich. Your prizes swell the hold.

ARION:

Spare me my life. I'll give you all my gold.

CAPTAIN:

When we reach Corinth gulf, the tides will shift;
You will retract your promise and your gift.
A forced gift is no gift —

ARION:

    Here, take this shell.
Your gift once saved my life; it served me well.
May it remind you of our earlier trust
Before that love was buried by gold dust.

CAPTAIN:

It's not my will. I have to mind my crew.

ARION:

And seal my murder?

CAPTAIN:

    What else can I do?

1ST MUTINEER:

You heard him.

2ND MUTINEER:

Kill yourself at once.

1ST MUTINEER:
If you want us to bury you on shore.

CAPTAIN:
What else can I do?

ARION:
Let me sing one last song before I die.

Arion goes up onto the afterdeck; the sailors all move forward to hear him.

ARION:
I do not wish to die. I fear to die,
To sink in the reflection of the sky,
At such a fearful depth to be alone,
To merge with shell and coral, slime and stone,
By tentacles caressed, by green fronds curled,
To drown myself in such a silent world.

My voice was loved, myself I cannot tell.
A hollow voice cried out from every shell.
Those who gave friendship I least understand
Who, when I needed love, let slip their hand.
But so it was, and I am glad I leave
No friends to mourn, no family to grieve.

O world so beautiful, grey olive trees,
Green laurel bushes, tempest-troubled seas,
I shall not see you or the clouds at night
Or the bright stars or sunset's golden light
Or smell the hyacinth or hear the cry
Of eagle or of wolf before I die.

His singing has an unsettling effect on the sailors. Some are deeply moved, others not. They start arguing. The scene becomes a riot. One sailor rushes to guard Arion with an oar or a sword, others attempt to charge him, only to be held off.

SAILORS:
Spare his life . . . Stop up his mouth . . . Throw him overboard . . . No! . . . Smash his lyre! . . . Jump – and die. *Ad lib.*

At the height of the clamour and chaos, Arion leaps off the ship into the waves.

Scene 6

A sea-change – a sudden silence – Arion is in the sea, sinking with
his lyre – he is under the waves –
> *The stars disappear above, the moon disappears. The blackness is*
> *complete.*
> *He is drowning and struggling and choking.*
> *Dolphin sounds. Phosphorescence.*
> *The beautiful swift trails of sea-beasts, including dolphins.*
> *He is buoyed up by dolphins, danced and played with; and carried*
> *along (holding a fin, riding on a dolphin's back) at a*
> *wonderfully rapid rate.*
> *Dolphin sounds: joyous.*
> *Arion believes that this exhilarating experience is death.*

ARION:
> The dark forgetful river
> That bounds the dead for ever,
> Transport me to that shore,
> For I fear death no more.

> Death was not hard and slow
> But soft and swift. I go
> Calm to that under-land
> Now joy has seized my hand.

The dolphin sounds become clearer, and among the clicks, cries, bubbling noises and so on are heard a few broken words, at first incoherently, then with high but clear articulation.

DOLPHIN:
Oh, no, no . . . no, no . . . [*clearer*] . . . musician –

ARION:
Yes?

DOLPHIN:
You are not . . .

ARION:
Not? I am not.

DOLPHIN:
. . . are not dead.

ARION:
Not what?

DOLPHIN:
Dead. Not dead.

ARION:
I am not dead? Why not?

DOLPHIN:
Dolphin. Dolphin.

ARION:
You are dolphins, yes, I see that . . .

DOLPHIN:
Music. Music.

ARION:
You want me to make more music?

DOLPHIN:
Music. We came to hear . . .

ARION:
To hear me sing? On the boat?

DOLPHIN:
On the boat. Then you leaped. And we saved you alive. We saved you alive. Alive. Alive.

ARION:
Please don't repeat everything. It's hard enough to take it all in once. You say I'm alive?

DOLPHIN *delightedly*:
Alive. Alive. Alive.

ARION:
I'm very grateful.
It's good of you.
Forgive me. I'm in shock.

DOLPHIN:
Alive . . . you are alive . . .

ARION:
And the ship?

DOLPHIN:
Sailed on, sailed on. We took you away. They did not see. They think you are dead. Your name, musician?

ARION:
Arion.

DOLPHIN:
Arion?

The dolphins sing the name's long vowels. They appear to like it.

ARION:
You dolphins seem to be susceptible to music.

DOLPHIN:
Very susceptible. Came to the ship. Lovely music. Saved a musician. Arion. Excellent dolphins.

ARION:
Excellent dolphins!
But aren't there evil dolphins too?

DOLPHIN:
Evil?

ARION:
Like the ones who tried to kidnap Dionysus the god of wine and sell him into slavery?

DOLPHIN:
Oh no, no, no – they were pirates, they were turned into dolphins. Bad as men, as dolphins good.
    Their descendants are good dolphins, and proud of their descent.

ARION *aside*:
How smug.

DOLPHIN:
A song. Listen.

He turned himself into a lion of gold
And round his head his golden eyes he rolled.
Ivy entwined the ship, and flutes were heard.
The oars, turned serpents, hissed each double word:
>Sleep, sleep,
>Leap, leap,
>Deep, deep.
The babbling pirates, leaping overboard,
Were smoothed to dolphins at a fluted chord.

A conch is heard.

ARION:
The conch!

DOLPHIN:
Listen!
That's the ship
From which you leapt.
We have overtaken it
And we will be in Corinth long before
The shell sounds on that shore.

ARION:
The shell, the gifted shell
That once was mine may be their supper bell.

DOLPHIN:
But now it's time for supper here as well.

*There is a feeding dance as the dolphins catch and pass and share and eat
fish – more like play than supper.*

ARION:
Raw fish!

DOLPHIN *dancing around in delighted attendance:*
Would you like some prawns? We could manage that. And
sea-spinach. But not eels, I'm afraid. My aunt died of a surfeit
of lampreys, and we've never had them on the table since.

Perhaps you'd like –

>A turbot,
>A burbot,
>A plate of plaice.
>A dab of dace.
A ling, a lobster, and a loach.
A roosterfish, a ray, a roach.
>A chub, a char,
>A grunt, a gar,
Three pilchards and a pound of parr.

DOLPHINS:
Fish give us a sufficiency
>Beneath the sea
>As you can see.
We eat with great efficiency
>Beneath the sea
>As you can see.

Like other good cetaceans
We scatter good vibrations.
We harry herring happily
And swallow salmon snappily.

Our skins are smooth and rubbery,
Our bulky bodies blubbery.
We harry herring happily
And swallow salmon snappily.

With unspecific gravity
And sinusoidal suavity
We harry herring happily
And swallow salmon snappily.

With aquabatic levity
And aerobatic brevity
We harry herring happily
And swallow salmon snappily.

ARION:
And doesn't anyone wish to eat you?

DOLPHIN:
Certain sharks try to get at young dolphins. And some
people – in the Black Sea, mainly. They salt us and eat us
later. And fishermen don't like us on the whole. We eat
their catch. And they kill us for that. Or we swim with the
shoals and get caught in their nets.

ARION:
That makes me doubly grateful that you saved me.

DOLPHIN:
You're not the first man led by us to shore.
Why, there were plenty more.

ARION:

Tell me about another.

DOLPHIN:

Icadius, Iapys' Cretan brother,
Shipwrecked, was guided by
A dolphin to Delphi;
And from that dolphin Delphi got its name:
Apollo and the dolphin were the same.

Or when Enalus saw his lover slung
Into the sea to calm the waves he flung
Himself into the waves that they might be
United constantly.
A dolphin saved him, and its mate his mate
From their too-fluid fate.

DOLPHIN:

You need to learn about our life and lore.
As your after-dinner task
Forget the world you've left and bask
In the warm rhythms of our dolphin masque.

An entertainment, a sort of masque, is laid on: scenes from dolphin life and lore, including some of the following:

Dolphin pairings and pods.
The dolphin life-cycle.
The dance of the dolphin midwives.
Conservation, pollution, netting, the killing of dolphins and other sea-life by man.
Hermit-dolphins who live apart from other dolphins.
Ambassador dolphins who make contact with humans.

Dolphins in the mythology and folklore of different cultures.
Dolphins as psychopomps, leading the souls of the human dead to the
underworld.
Defence against sharks: dolphins ram them with their snouts.
Dolphin sonar: dolphins close their eyes and can still catch fish.
Sleeplessness: dolphins never sleep since they need to come up to the
surface for air; half their brains rest at a time.
True stories from around the world of humans being rescued by
dolphins.

The other sea-creatures also appear and act their parts in the masque:
fronds, anemones, sharks, globefish, abalone, corals, conches, herring,
salmon, sea-horses, electric eels, plankton, whales – perhaps a friendly
jellyfish, who likes touching other beasts and can't understand why he's
shunned.

The dolphins perform a joyful dance for Arion.

DOLPHINS:

    Round and round, round and round,
    Leaping up and plunging down,
    Fins and flippers flying free,
    We dolphins dart around the sea.

ARION:

    What joyful lives you dolphins lead
    Both when you mate and when you feed.
    Compare it to my own condition –
    A poor, unhappy, flipperless musician.

DOLPHIN:

Oh, no –
You interest us, we interest you.
And we can tell who's who.
And we like music too.
We have our ancient musical traditions.
That's why we are susceptible to musicians.
Perhaps we should sing together after supper.
You take the lower part, I'll take the upper.

They sing a duet, the dolphin singing open vowels, Arion doing the same as well as playing the lyre. Soon the voices of dolphin and human are wonderfully intertwined.

DOLPHIN:

I love Arion, and would like to be
Bound to his voice and him eternally.

The other dolphins leave one by one, and Arion and the dolphin are left swimming towards Corinth.

ARION:

The days pass one by one.
I feel my life has only just begun –
And, for the first time, I am having fun!

ARION *and* DOLPHIN:

In air and water both, our voices part and blend,
And I/you, who never sought a friend
Have found one in the end.

Scene 7

Fisherfolk gather on the shore.

FISHERMAN:
Look – look – in the Gulf –

FISHERMAN:
A dolphin and a young man with a lyre –

FISHERMAN:
They'll get caught in our nets –

FISHERMAN:
Save him –

FISHERMAN:
No, no – they've swum under them –

FISHERMAN:
It is Arion.

FISHERMAN:
No!

FISHERMAN:
Let's inform the court.

FISHERMAN:
Let Periander know.

They go off to inform Periander.

ARION:

> Now, Dolphin, you must go,
> My part is here above, and yours below —
> I where the winds, you where the waters flow.
> It must be so.
>
> How said I am that I must part
> From the dolphin of my heart!

DOLPHIN:

> With you I will remain —
> For if we part we'll never meet again
> And I would die of loneliness and pain.
> This I maintain.

Periander and his guards arrive.

During this scene, the fisherfolk, quite delighted with the dolphin, prod it with their oars out of interest, and keep it apart. The dolphin is a little bewildered and frightened.

Meanwhile, Periander draws Arion out of the water.

PERIANDER:

Arion! Arion!

ARION:

My lord, my friend the dolphin —

PERIANDER:

What is this?
Arion, you're alive. You won?
Get that dolphin away —

ARION:

But, my lord . . .

PERIANDER:

When did you return?
How did you fare in Sicily? What did you sing?
Where are your prizes?

ARION:

My lord, my friend the dolphin saved my life.

PERIANDER:

What do you mean?
Don't speak in riddles.
Come out of there. At once. You're cold and wet.
Where's the ship? The Captain?

ARION:

They saw my gold and forced me overboard.
The dolphin saved me, fed me, brought me here.
And now insists on staying on, my lord,
Unawed by fate, by foreignness, by fear.

PERIANDER:

I see. Where are the Captain and the crew?
Speak, speak at once! How can I credit you?
I never heard of anything more strange
Than your strange history of chance and change.
Prove, prove your clever story if you can.
The Captain is a highly trusted man.

ARION:

I trusted him, my lord – and half my grief
Is for my lost belief.
It is the bitter truth that I have told.
I won in Sicily. They stole my gold.

PERIANDER:

Where is the ship? Where is the crew?
Where is my proof?

ARION:

My lord, what shall I do?

PERIANDER:

You say the dolphin wishes to remain.
How would you know? Explain at once. Explain!

ARION:

We spoke, my lord –

PERIANDER:

Spoke? Spoke? Spoke to that wretched fish?
Then let it speak again. It is my wish
The dolphin speak. Command it so to do
That I may hear this dolphin language too.
If the beast speaks, throw it a mackerel.
I, Periander, wait. Speak now! Speak well!
Speak! Speak!

The dolphin does not speak.
   Periander becomes more and more suspicious.
   Suddenly he turns to the guards and indicates Arion.

Arrest him. Take him away!

FISHERFOLK:

But, my lord, what about the dolphin?

PERIANDER:

Oh – do what you like with the dolphin –

50

The guards drag Arion off.

The fisherfolk turn the dolphin into a sort of circus act. They force it through hoops, make it leap for dead fish, collect money for it.

FISHERFOLK:
Roll up, roll up, roll up, and see the dolphin play.
Free for the under-fives. Half-price on Saturday.

Scene 8

Arion wakes up in his prison cell. Through the bars he looks up at the night sky. The messenger enters.

MESSENGER:
Arion of Lesbos, I am required by Periander, Tyrant of Corinth, to inform you that the dolphin is dead.

Arion starts. There is a look of horror on his face. The messenger continues:

The dolphin wasted away
From day to day . . .
It glutted and it groaned.
It squealed, it moaned.
'Arion . . . Arion . . .' all day long
It seemed to say – a high, pathetic song.
Into its misery the creature sank.
Ringed by dead fish it stank.

Arion groans with misery.

PERIANDER *who has been standing outside:*
Ah, how I grieve
That I kept them apart. It is too late,
And I have earned his endless hate.

He enters the prison cell.

Arion – forgive me –
You did not feign that cry.
Forgive me that the dolphin had to die.
You are free. You are free. Open the prison gate.
The dolphin's tomb will be erected by the state.

Periander marches out. The guards remove the bars from around Arion.

ARION *who has taken in nothing of all this*:
  Alone am I, and sad that you are dead,
  That you are dead, not I –
  That you were kind to me and that led you to die.
  When all is done and said –
  When all is said and done,
  You were my friend, the only one.

Scene 9

The full chorus (everyone except the Captain and the sailors) enters in candle-lit procession. A tomb is built for the dolphin, beneath a dark, starless sky.

CHILDREN'S CHORUS *and* FULL CHORUS:
Now the sun is setting
And the night is near,
Look down on our city,
Keep us safe from fear.

Till the hour of sunrise
Let our labours cease.
May our sleep be dreamless.
May we rest in peace –

Farmers in the mountains,
Sailors on the waves,
All who suffer sadness,
All who rest in graves.

Now the sun is setting
And the night is near,
Look down on our city,
Keep us safe from fear.

ARION:

    Day follows night, night day.

    Try as I wish, I cannot keep away.

    Night follows day, day night.

    I watch myself mourn from a distant height.

    I sing in my own voice, but in the end,

    The voice is yours, my friend.

    Why did you have to die?

    Why? Why? Why? Why?

    I ask, I ask, and there is no reply.

CHILDREN'S CHORUS *to Arion*:

    Till the light of morning

    Let your mourning cease.

    May your sleep be dreamless.

    May you rest in peace.

Arion sleeps, exhausted, behind the tomb. The distant sound of a conch is heard.

    The Captain and sailors come up from the shore, bearing flaming torches.

    Periander comes forward.

PERIANDER:

Welcome, Captain; home at last, I see.

CAPTAIN:

Thanks to your lordship's prayers to the gods –

Though I have yet to see my home and wife –

PERIANDER:

The gods, yes, yes; a happy voyage, I hope?

CAPTAIN:

We carry merchandise from Italy –
Detailed in full, of course, at the customs house.

PERIANDER:

Excellent, excellent. But where's Arion?

CAPTAIN:

He won at the Sicilian festival.
All present praised him, and he gained great gifts –
But midway in our voyage came a ship
That claimed to go to Lesbos, and he too,
Longing to see his native coast once more,
Transferred his gold and sailed away from us.

PERIANDER:

Why do you weep that he was fortunate?

CAPTAIN:

I weep because I must.

PERIANDER:

        My gentle Captain –
Swear on your mother's womb that this is true.
Swear on the dolphin's tomb that this is true.
Swear that you do not lie.
Swear, that you may not die.
Swear, all of you.

CAPTAIN:

What dolphin's tomb, my lord?

57

PERIANDER:

This tomb that it has pleased the state
To raise. Swear, swear. Why do you hesitate?

The sailors swear, placing their palms on the tomb. The Captain cannot.
Arion awakes. The sailors see him and are struck dumb with horror.
They tremble, and try to run, but are held by the guards.
The Captain turns around in amazement. Torn between relief and
shock, he moves towards Arion and says, with unmistakable joy:

CAPTAIN:

Arion –
Alive!
The gods be praised.
I have been thinking of you night and day.

Arion turns away from him.

Those nights and days
I have not slept
Upon the sea.
Your voice has crept
Through my heart's maze
To torture me.

SAILORS:

It's not the gods
But our own hearts
We need to fear.
The evil starts
Against all odds
Not there but here.

PERIANDER:

Take him away.

58

CAPTAIN:

    Tyrant, my ship is like your city.

    I sacrificed, suppressing pity,

    An innocent man. I was to blame.

    You, Tyrant, would have done the same.

PERIANDER:

I've heard enough.

Put him and all his ruffians to the sword.

ARION:

Let them go, my lord.

PERIANDER:

Arion, do not raise your voice.

They compassed death. I have no choice.

ARION:

Defer their sentence for a day –

An hour, my lord – and hear me play.

Perhaps my words will draw your bitterness away.

PERIANDER:

Play, then, Arion, and sing.

I, who have caused you grief, am listening.

Arion turns to the Captain and in a gesture of reconciliation takes the conch-shell once more and holds it to his ear. The sounds of the sea are heard, and the cries of dolphins.

ARION:

    I hear your voice sing out my name by night,

        By dawn, by evening light.

I mourn for you, yet, Dolphin, to my shame,
 I never asked your name.

Your element protected me, but mine
 For you proved far too fine.

Dolphin, it was from your marine caress
 That I learned gentleness.

May music bind the sky, the earth, the sea
 In tune, in harmony.

Dark sea, protect all voyagers whose home
 Rests in your ring of foam.

Warm earth, teach us to nourish, not destroy
 The souls that give us joy.

Bright stars, engrave my dolphin and my lyre
 In the night sky with fire.

The northern constellations of Delphinus and Lyra appear in the night sky.

END